The Dust of Butterfly Wings

As a boy growing up on a hillside farm in southwest Missouri near Purdy, Eddie spent much of his time clearing new ground and raising strawberries. His parents taught him to be honest, work hard and treat people with respect. His interests include motivational speaking, inspirational teaching, and entertaining. For several years he has been a comedian on the Brumley music show in Branson, Missouri. He is also a song writer, musician and writer of inspirational and children's books.

Eddie and his wife, Evelyn, have four children and five grandchildren.

Eddie loves to tell stories of humor and common sense with practical applications for everyday life. He brings laughter and encouragement to readers and audiences of all ages.

The Dust of Butterfly Wings

By

Eddie Bowman

Illustrated by

Jane Lenoir

Bowman Publishing, Inc.
154 Whispering Oaks Drive
Galena, MO 65656
1-888-336-5132 or (417) 272-8839

Library of Congress cataloging-in-publication data

Bowman, Eddie D., 1939-
    The dust of butterfly wings / by Eddie Bowman ;
    illustrated by Jane Lenoir.
        p.   cm.
    Summary: Although he doesn't understand his
    wise Chief's advice as to how to become the
    strongest, swiftest runner in the tribe, Mighty Bear
    follows the counsel with determination.
        ISBN 1-931281-30-0 (cloth).
        -- ISBN 1-931281-31-9 (pbk.)
        1. Indians of North America—Juvenile fiction.
    [1. Indians of NorthAmerica—Fiction. 2
    Determination
    (Personality trait)—Fiction.]   I. Lenoir, Jane, 1950-
    ill. II. Title.
    IN PROCESS
    [Fic]—dc21   96-54229
                                              CIP
                                               AC

iv

Contents

Dedicated to

my grand-daughter Jennifer Lea Gould

Chapter 1

The Secret

Mighty Bear was a young boy of a Native American tribe who lived long, long ago. One day he went to the tribe chief, Elk Horn, and told him he wanted to grow up to be the fastest runner and strongest brave in the entire tribe.

"What can I do?" asked Mighty Bear.

The wise old chief said, "Mighty Bear, if you want to be swift and strong, cover your heart with the dust of butterfly wings."

"Why?" asked Mighty Bear. "Is there magic in the dust? I don't understand."

Chief Elk Horn replied, "Mighty Bear, you don't have to understand. You just need to believe. Just do as I say. Cover your heart with the dust of butterfly wings, and you will become the strongest, fastest runner in the entire tribe."

Mighty Bear was overjoyed! He said, "I will start chasing butterflies today!"

The chief said, "Mighty Bear, no matter what anyone says, you must keep on believing. Some of your friends will laugh at you and think you're crazy, but you keep right on catching butterflies every day, especially the big ones, for they are the best. And if anyone asks you why, just tell them the chief knows. And Mighty Bear, don't tell anyone your secret until you become chief. Then you can tell."

Mighty Bear was so excited he could hardly speak! "Did you say I will be a chief someday?" Mighty Bear stammered.

"Yes," answered Chief Elk Horn. "Run along, now, Mighty Bear, you have a lot to do. And remember, I'm here if you ever need me."

"Oh, thank you," said the young man. "I will keep on believing no matter what. Thank you, thank you!"

As Mighty Bear hurried away, the old chief thought back many moons ago when he was a young boy himself. I see myself in that young man, he thought. I had the same desires, and my chief told me the same things. I'm glad at last that I can pass on the secret to someone like Mighty Bear.

Chapter 2

Buffalo Horns

When Mighty Bear got home, his mother, Pretty Star, noticed something different about him. She said, "Son, where have you been? And why are you smiling so?"

"Oh, I've been talking to the chief," he said, trying to hide his excitement. But he did not tell her what they had talked about. "Have you seen my bow and arrows?" Mighty Bear asked. "I want to go to the woods for a while. Maybe I can get us a rabbit or squirrel for supper."

"Mighty Bear," his mother answered, "your bow and arrows are right where you left them yesterday, remember?"

But he could not remember. His mother said, "I'll give you a clue. Buffalo horns."

"Oh, that's right," Mighty Bear said

as he remembered. Just below their village was a spring. A large white oak tree stood on the bank near the water. Mighty Bear's uncle, Swift Eagle, had come in from a hunting trip and brought Mighty Bear a huge set of buffalo horns. Mighty Bear tied them to the white oak tree with buckskin straps. There was a big knot on the tree that resembled a man's face. It had eyes, a nose, and a mouth. Mighty Bear had even made some paint to color

the face. Now, with these horns sticking out of its head, it really looked scary!

"Thanks, Mother, for reminding me," he said. "I'll be back in a little while."

"Be careful!" she warned. "And bring me back a fat rabbit for supper." As Mighty Bear approached the oak tree he saw the scary head with the buffalo horns. Mighty Bear was proud of himself for this work of art. He thought, If I didn't know what that was, it would scare me to death! He walked around the tree and found his bow leaning against the tree with six arrows right where he had left them. I'll leave them here for now and pick them up on my way back, he told himself. Then he began walking near the spring branch, looking not for rabbits or squirrels, but for butterflies!

Chapter 3

Chasing Butterflies

Catching butterflies, Mighty Bear soon learned, was not the easiest thing in the world to do. He found a lot of little blue butterflies along the banks and shallow mudholes. They were pretty easy to catch. But their wings were small, and they didn't have very much dust on them. He caught a few anyway and wiped the dust across his bare chest. But he remembered what the chief had said, "The big ones are the very best!"

So he began searching for the big ones. Soon a large one flew up from a flower right in front of him! Mighty Bear began chasing it. About the time he thought he would catch it, it would dart away from him. But no matter how hard he tried, it always got away. Then he found other large butterflies. He ran as hard and fast as he could. Up hills, down hills, through the woods, and across open fields, Mighty Bear ran everywhere!

Finally, almost by accident, he caught a large one! He rubbed the dust across his heart as he said, "I Believe!" He flexed his muscles and pounded his chest and said, "I feel stronger already!"

Then he returned to the oak tree by the spring, picked up his bow and arrows, and headed back up the hill to the village. A fat rabbit hopped across the path in front of him and stood motionless near a clump of blackberry vines. Mighty Bear stopped and very carefully placed an arrow in his bow, drew back the arrow, took aim, and released it. The arrow hit a small limb of a blackjack tree and missed the rabbit. Oh, no! he thought. Mother wanted rabbit for supper, and it's too late now for me to get one!

Then he heard his mother calling him, "Mighty Bear, where are you?"

When they met in the path, it was getting dark.

"Where have you been?" she asked. "You have been gone forever!"

"Oh, I'm sorry," he replied, "but I didn't know it was getting so late. I've been gone all this time, and I didn't even get a rabbit. But tomorrow I'll get one for you, I promise!"

"Tomorrow," Pretty Star said, "we're working in the corn and beans. There will be no time for hunting."

Mighty Bear knew that if there were no time for hunting, there would be no time for butterflies, either! But at least he had made a start, and as he lay down to sleep, he was careful not to rub the dust off his chest. Maybe this dust will work through the night, he thought, as he quickly fell asleep.

The next morning, Pretty Star called Mighty Bear for breakfast. He opened his eyes and looked at his chest where there was still a trace of the butterfly dust. "I believe," he mumbled, as he put on his moccasins.

"You believe what?" his mother asked.

Alarmed that his mother had heard him, he said, "I believe . . . uh . . . uh . . . I believe . . . I will . . . uh . . . put on my moccasins!"

She said, "Mighty Bear, are you all right? You already have your moccasins on! Are you awake? Are you OK?"

He said, "I'm fine, Mother, but I sure am hungry."

"Well, I can fix that," she replied. "You just come and see what we have for breakfast. And you'd better eat plenty! We have a lot of work to do today."

After their meal, Mighty Bear went to the field with his mother and his brothers and sisters. Some of his cousins, uncles, and aunts went, too.

As they hoed the corn and pulled the weeds, Mighty Bear could hardly keep his mind on his work. Once in a while, he would see a butterfly going from one wildflower to another sipping nectar. He wanted to chase it so badly, but was afraid he would get into trouble if he did. But finally, the temptation was too great. While the other workers were on the other end of the field, a large butterfly flew in front of him, and he leaped out to catch it. The butterfly went zigzagging across the cornfield with Mighty Bear right behind it! He was so intent on catching it, he paid no attention to anything else. And before he realized what he had done, he came face to face with his mother!

"Mighty Bear!" she shouted. "Have you lost your mind? Look at all the corn you stepped on! What in the world are you doing? You're supposed to be killing weeds, not corn! Now give an account for yourself!"

Poor Mighty Bear didn't know what to say. "Oh, just chasing that pretty butterfly," he uttered.

"Chasing a butterfly!" his mother exclaimed. "In the cornfield? That's ridiculous! Now you get back to work, and this had better never happen again!"

He slowly turned around and walked back to the other end of the field. His cousins, who saw his wild romp through the corn, teased him all day about it. They even made up a little rhyme about him.

"Mighty Bear, Mighty Bear, he was born
To chase big butterflies through the corn.
To run and play and step on plants,
And leave the work to uncles and aunts!"

But the more they teased him, the harder he worked. Under his breath he said, "I Believe!" About that time, Chief Elk Horn passed by. He heard the teasing, and as he walked by, he winked at Mighty Bear. That was all he needed. Mighty Bear pulled more weeds than anyone! And as he worked, he chanted to himself his own little rhyme,

"Mighty Bear, Mighty Bear, I was born
To be tougher than a buffalo horn.
To grow strong and tall like corn and beans,
Thanks to the dust of butterfly wings!"

15

Chapter 4

Growing Stronger

Chief Elk Horn was very pleased as he watched Mighty Bear's progress. Actually, everybody noticed how strong and swift he was becoming. But Pretty Star became more and more concerned about her son. Oh, there was no problem getting him to work. He worked harder than anybody else. And if anyone in the tribe needed help in lifting logs or rocks or animals they had killed, they always called on Mighty Bear because he was so strong. But his mother could not understand why he was gone so much and why he preferred to hunt alone. He usually brought back some animal to eat, but she kept noticing the dust on his chest, and she asked him why he was still chasing butterflies. He tried to change the subject, but she kept pressing him, so he said, "The chief knows."

She had noticed that Mighty Bear had been spending a lot of time with the chief. She thought that he might be troubled. So finally, she went to the chief herself and told him of Mighty Bear's behavior and of her concern.

"Now, Pretty Star," said the chief, "don't you worry about Mighty Bear. Yes, I know all about the dust of butterfly wings, but that is a little secret between Mighty Bear and me. You just let him go. You're going to be proud of him."

From that day on, Pretty Star never questioned Mighty Bear about his hunting trips or the dust on his chest. As the new moons came and went, Mighty Bear became stronger and swifter. Chasing butterflies up and down the hills, across the river bottoms, and through the fields was giving him exercise that others did not get. He remembered how, at first, it was almost impossible to catch a large butterfly, but now it was becoming easier. Sometimes he wondered if the dust had

18

anything at all to do with his increasing skills. Was it the strenuous exercise alone that made the difference? Yet the chief said, "Cover your heart with the dust of butterfly wings. Keep on believing. You will become the strongest, fastest runner in the entire tribe." So Mighty Bear continued this practice day after day and realized that Chief Elk Horn's promise was coming true.

Chapter 5

Saving a White Boy

About thirty miles from the natives' village was a small white settlement. They had a trading post, a general mercantile store, a hardware store, a blacksmith shop, a community church, and a country doctor. The blacksmith, Albert Potter, had a son, Willard, who was two years younger than Mighty Bear. They became the best of friends. Mighty Bear was interested in wagons, carriages, horses, and farm implements. He learned much from Willard. Willard was interested in hunting, fishing, and the ways of the wilderness. He learned much from Mighty Bear.

One day, the two had agreed to meet at noon beneath a great sycamore tree on the big river, just two miles from the white village. Mighty Bear left his village at daylight so he could catch butterflies on the way. When he arrived, Willard was not there yet, so he continued catching butterflies while keeping within sight of the sycamore tree.

Shortly, he heard a desperate call for help! He raced to the river crossing and saw Willard rolling on the gravel bar while holding his leg in great pain!

"Mighty Bear!" he called. "You've got to help me! Quick! I've been bitten by a cottonmouth moccasin!"

Mighty Bear quickly ripped Willard's shirt and made a tourniquet and tied it tightly around Willard's leg, just above his knee. Then he took his knife and made tiny cuts where the fangs had entered and sucked out some of the poison. But he knew that Willard had to have medicine in a hurry or he would die! Already his leg was swelling and he was deathly sick! Every minute was critical! Mighty Bear picked up Willard in his strong arms.

"Where are we going!" screamed Willard.

"To your doctor," replied Mighty Bear.

"But you can't carry me that far!" shrieked Willard.

"You just watch me, Willard!" said Mighty Bear. "Don't worry about me. We'll make it. You just hang on!" He ran as fast as he could to the white village! A few times he was so nearly exhausted that he felt he would faint, but then, the words of the chief would come to his head, "Keep on believing!"

"Willard!" he shouted. "I believe! I believe! You must believe, also! We're almost there, Willard. Hang on!"

Mighty Bear burst into the doctor's office and laid Willard down on the floor.

The surprised doctor said, "What is going on here?"

Mighty Bear was gasping for breath as he said, "Here!" pointing to the swollen leg. "Snakebite . . . cottonmouth! Hurry!"

The doctor said, "Oh, my word! Willard, can you hear me?" Willard was barely conscious, but the doctor heard him faintly say, "Yes, I believe, too!"

While the doctor worked over Willard, Mighty Bear, getting back his breath, ran down the street to the blacksmith shop. Mr. Potter was shaping some horseshoes in the forge when Mighty Bear shouted, "Mr. Potter! Come quick! Willard . . . at doctor!"

Mr. Potter dropped the red-hot

horseshoes in the tub of water and raced to the doctor's office! "What is it? What's wrong?" he shouted as he entered the room.

The doctor said, "Albert, just calm down. Everything is going to be all right. Your boy, Willard, got a nasty bite from a cottonmouth, but thanks to Mighty Bear, he's gonna make it. Five minutes longer and he would have been gone!"

Mr. Potter put his hands on Mighty Bear's broad shoulders and his eyes filled with tears. His voice quivered as he said, "Mighty Bear, you saved Willard's life. I can never repay you. You will be my friend forever."

Mighty Bear bade Willard farewell and went back to his own village. It was early in the morning when he approached the spring and home. The dust of butter-fly wings, he said to himself. Yes, I do believe!

Chapter 6

Saving His Own People

News spread quickly throughout both native and white communities about Mighty Bear's strength and speed that saved a white boy. And it would not be long until his skills would be put to the test again, this time to save his own people. There was a place about ten miles away where wild turkey were plentiful. Mighty Bear loved wild turkey, especially the way his mother prepared it. But somebody else loved turkey, too. She was a beautiful young maiden named Little Fawn. If Mighty Bear got a turkey, perhaps Little Fawn would come over and they could eat together. Somehow, he had never noticed before just how pretty and sweet she was.

On this cool, crisp morning, as Mighty Bear made preparations for his turkey hunt, he stopped at the spring for a drink of water. Little Fawn was there.

"Little Fawn!" he exclaimed. "What are you doing here so early in the morning?"

She said, "I heard you were going to hunt turkey today. I just wanted to wish you good luck." She leaned over and placed a kiss on Mighty Bear's cheek. He was so shy that he didn't know what to say, but, oh, how thrilled he was at this sign of affection! He knew now that she liked him just as he liked her.

Finally, he said, "Thank you, Little

Fawn, for being here this morning. I am going after the biggest turkey in the woods! When I get back, we'll eat turkey together!" As he left the spring, he looked over his shoulder and waved at Little Fawn. He thought back to the time many moons ago when he caught his first butterfly and how he was so careful not to rub off the dust from his chest. Now, he was careful not to rub the kiss from his cheek.

Mighty Bear was in no hurry to get to the turkey woods. Since butterflies were plentiful, he spent a lot of time chasing them. He planned to sleep out that night in the woods so he could hunt the turkeys early the next morning.

The day passed quickly. He realized he must find the right place to camp because the sun was now setting. He found a nice flat area near the path and made his camp. As he sat in the woods, he thought about turkeys and butterflies and Little Fawn. He reached down and felt the fresh butterfly dust on his chest, then with the other hand, he touched his cheek where Little Fawn had kissed him. He felt like he was about the luckiest person in the world as he drifted off to sleep.

Mighty Bear had been asleep for a few hours when he was awakened by the sound of low voices. Rising slowly, he looked across the hollow to the next ridge. He knew the path circled to the area of the voices so he crept silently along the path. As he began to climb to the top of the ridge, he saw the light of a small campfire and the figures of men. He sneaked a little closer.. Then peering through the under-brush, he saw a band of war braves, about twenty in number. He knew they were from an enemy tribe. He heard the name of his own tribe mentioned a number of times. While he could understand only parts of the conversation, he quickly put the pieces together. These war braves were planning a surprise attack on the village by the spring at daybreak! And that was only three hours away. He knew he had to act fast, yet quietly!

Under the full moon, he could see

the steep and winding path back to the village. When he was far enough away from the braves that he knew he could not be heard, he began to run at full speed. The braves would not be far behind! Never had he needed strength and speed as he did now! And again, as when he saved the white boy, there were times he felt he could not go on. But then he remembered the dust of butterfly wings and also Little Fawn's warm kiss. "I believe, I believe!" he gasped as he pushed on with all his might.

Arriving at the village about half an hour before daylight, he quickly awakened everyone. The warriors grabbed their bows and arrows and hid themselves in the rocks and cliffs near the spring! A few quiet moments passed. Then they saw the war party sneaking up the path toward the spring. But suddenly, the intruders came to a dead stop! It was just light enough for them to see the eerie face with the buffalo horns at the big oak tree. They were frightened by it! Then, the men from the rocks let their arrows fly against the war braves! They were so frightened and caught off guard, they turned around and fled!

Mighty Bear had saved his own people with his strength and speed! They put

Mighty Bear on their shoulders and carried him up the hill to the village. Everyone came out to meet them. They all shouted words of thanks to Mighty Bear!

"Oh, it was nothing," he said. Then he said to himself, "Except the dust of butterfly wings . . ." Then looking over and seeing Little Fawn, he added, "And the kiss of Little Fawn! Oh, how I believe!"

Chapter 7

Greater Tests and Victories

Mighty Bear's reputation as a strong, swift brave grew and spread. Everyone was talking now! The chief was so proud of him! But Chief Elk Horn knew that Mighty Bear must be careful and not be overconfident. So he met him one morning at the spring and said, "Mighty Bear, I am so pleased with your progress, but I must warn you that there are other tests to come! If you meet these trials successfully, you will become a chief. Then, when the time is right, you can reveal your secret!"

Mighty Bear wanted to talk more, but the chief seemed tired and weary, so he didn't ask for any more of his time. As he thought on the words of the chief, Little Fawn appeared. Oh, she was pretty! And they were so much in love! Their parents were making plans now for their marriage in the fall.

"Little Fawn," he said as he held her by the hand, "I never did get you that turkey! Tomorrow, I'll go back and get the biggest turkey in the woods just for you!"

Little Fawn replied, "And I will be here at the spring in the morning to wish you good luck!"

He knew what that meant! He couldn't wait!

The next morning, Little Fawn was there for him. "Good luck," she said as she kissed Mighty Bear.

As he left, he remembered the last time he had gone turkey hunting and the narrow escape with enemies. He hoped that this time would be much different. Yet he could not forget the words of the chief, "Greater tests will come." But Mighty Bear believed. With the dust of butterfly wings on his chest and the sweet kiss of Little Fawn on his lips, he felt like he could meet any test. Little did he know just how hard those tests would be or how soon they would come.

Mighty Bear walked for several miles and stirred up a bunch of large butterflies. He began chasing them with great energy, eager to spread their fresh dust on his heart. He followed those butterflies in places he had never been. Up and down, around and around he went. Then stopping to get his directions, suddenly he realized that he was lost! He had no idea where the path was or how far it might be! After a few moments of rest and careful thought, he began walking in what he believed was the right direction to the path. But the further he walked, the more confused he became! He didn't see anything that looked familiar! He came to a spring he had never seen. He drank of the cool, refreshing water.

He walked on, but was soon overtaken by darkness. The wind started blowing while dark clouds with thunder, lightning, and rain moved in! He managed to find a crevice in a large boulder on the side of the hill that gave him some protection from the storm. Limbs were falling all around him because of the strong winds. It was the worst storm he could remember. It seemed that it would never end!

But finally, the woods were quiet again, except for the dripping of the water from the trees and the familiar sounds of wild animals. Mighty Bear was wet and cold. How glad he was when the warm sunshine of morning at last appeared. Having laid down his bow and arrows and other belongings when he started chasing butterflies, he faced some difficulties. He found some edible roots and ripe berries which tasted wonderful! After eating, he began walking again, hoping to find his way home. He broke through a thicket of hazel brush and found himself standing in a path.

In a matter of seconds, he was completely surrounded by unfriendly natives! They asked him his name and tribe. He told them. Immediately, two warriors grabbed him and tied his hands with straps! Mighty Bear soon realized that this was the enemy tribe that had planned to take their village, and the braves realized Mighty Bear was the brave with the reputation for such great strength and speed! Mighty Bear told them he meant no harm, that he was not spying on them, but that he had simply gotten lost and was looking for his way home.

They took him to their village and tied him to a stake. Everyone stared at him.

The chief called for his strongest brave. There were three huge stones lying nearby, and he ordered his brave to lift them. He lifted the first two but could not lift the third one. Then turning to Mighty Bear he said, "You try."

Mighty Bear lifted the first stone and set it down. Then he lifted the second stone. A butterfly had landed on the third stone. He caught the butterfly and, in one sweeping motion, brushed his heart. No one really noticed. "I believe!" he said, as he lifted the third stone. With a mighty heave, he brought it to his chest and let it go with a thud! The natives applauded him.

The chief was greatly impressed. Then he called for his fastest runner. He said, "Tomorrow, you shall race Swift Deer."

Mighty Bear was taken back to the stake where he spent another night. He was given little to eat, yet he felt ready for the race.

"Other tests will come," his own chief had said. "If you meet these tests successfully, you will become a chief. Then when the time is right, you can reveal your secret." All these thoughts went through his mind as well as sweet thoughts of Little Fawn.

When morning came, the whole tribe gathered for the race. Mighty Bear and Swift Deer stood side by side. The chief gave the signal and they sprang forward. Mighty Bear slipped a little and fell behind! But once he gained his footing, with a burst of energy, he passed Swift Deer and reached the finish line ahead of him! They all shouted and applauded him. The chief said that he had never seen such speed and strength.

Having great respect now for Mighty Bear, the chief said, "We must take him home and make peace with his people! Mighty Bear, we know now that the stories are true we have heard about you. We want to be your friend! Take us to your chief so we can make peace!"

That night they gave Mighty Bear

the best of everything they had. Then, when morning came, they began their journey to the village by the spring.

"Is there anything you need?" the chief asked.

"Just one thing," replied Mighty Bear. "I'll show you on the way home."

It was about the middle of the next afternoon when the party arrived at the village. Approaching the spring, they saw the scary head with buffalo horns which had frightened them before.

As they were drinking at the spring, Mighty Bear looked up and saw Little Fawn running toward him! "Mighty Bear!" she called. He ran to meet her. "I've been so worried about you," she said. "I'm so glad you're home, but who are these men?"

Mighty Bear said, "These are warriors from a neighboring tribe. They have come to make peace with our people. They are asking for our chief."

Little Fawn hung her head and said

sadly, "Chief Elk Horn died last night. But he told us that when you came back, we were to make you chief!"

They walked on up to the village, and everyone shouted for joy when they saw Mighty Bear. In a solemn ceremony, Mighty Bear was made chief. The first thing he did was to make a peace treaty with the braves who had brought him home.

"And now," Mighty Bear said, "there is one thing else we need to do. Swift Deer, will you bring me the turkey?" Mighty Bear had asked the braves to stop in the turkey woods on the way to help him find the biggest turkey in the woods. Then he went to Little Fawn's side and said, "Little Fawn, you wished me good luck when I went to find a turkey for you. Good luck has finally come. For here we are with a fine turkey to eat, we are at peace with our enemies, and tomorrow, you and I will be married!" Everyone whooped and hollered for joy!

Chapter 8

Passing On the Secret

As the years passed, Mighty Bear and Little Fawn lived happily and raised children of their own. One morning, Mighty Bear was standing at the spring thinking back to the many things that had happened during his lifetime.

A young boy, Running Dog, approached him and said, "Chief Mighty Bear, could I ask you a question?"

"Sure," the chief replied.

The boy said, "Chief, I want to be the strongest, fastest runner in the entire tribe. Can you tell me what to do?"

Chief Mighty Bear realized, at last, the time was right to reveal his secret. The chief replied, "Yes, I can tell you what to do, Running Dog, if you really believe."

"Oh, I will believe anything you tell me!" said the eager young man.

"OK," the chief replied, "now listen carefully, Running Dog. If you want to be the strongest, fastest runner in the entire tribe, cover your heart with the dust of butterfly wings."

The End